Roger Stevens

illustrated by Spike Gerrell

BLOOMSBURY EDUCATION
AN IMPRINT OF BLOOMSBURY

LONDON OXFORD NEW YORK NEW DELHI SYDNEY

CONTENTS

Introduction

Welcome to *Is This a Poem?* Now, that might sound like an easy question. But it's not. When we read a poem with a regular rhyme, with regular lines, set out in a regular way, then most of us recognise it as a poem. And most of us know what a poem isn't – it isn't a story or a newspaper article, or a feature in a magazine. But what about those many other forms of writing that exist in between those examples? How about:

Jack and Jill went up the hill
to fetch a pail of water.
Jack fell down and broke his crown
and Jill came tumbling after.

Is that a poem or just a silly rhyme for young children?

Is a football chant a poem? Are the lyrics to songs poetry?

In this book I'll be looking at all the different and more unusual ways poets like to use words to make poems, from ancient haiku poetry to modern verses written by poets who love to play around with words.

Part 1: When Is A Poem Not A Poem?

In my book *What Rhymes With Sneeze?* I looked at all kinds of poems that rhymed. There will be a few rhyming poems in this book, but most of the poems won't rhyme.

And it's when words don't rhyme that things get tricky. Did you know that sometimes even great poets and scholars can't agree on what poetry actually is? It's true. So here are a few poems to whet your appetite. Or *are* they poems? I think they are. But what do *you* think?

Not a Poem

This poem is not a kite
it doesn't long to float on wind
no girl held it
no boy lost it
you can't deny it has no string.

This poem is not a bird
it doesn't want a song to sing
no man heard it
no woman watched it
it cannot fly, it has no wings.

This poem is not a star
it doesn't light the sky by night
no one can follow it
no child wished on it
it's never seen, shining bright.

This poem is not a poem
it doesn't dream, it's merely lines
no one can love it
no one should say it
it's only words and clever rhymes.

Sue Hardy-Dawson

Cleaning My Room is Out of the Question

From this historic spot
    between the ancient pizza
    and the festering sock
    just here beneath the homework diary
(that I told you I had lost)
the alien invasion of our planet has begun.

They came from inner space
    from milkshake mugs
    and lolly wrappers
    from bubblegum and spit
new life forms – grey-green velvet, humpy, wriggly things.

They may be small now
    smears of furry slime
    fuzzy blobs of gloop
    with crispy fringes
but they'll grow.

They'll grow.

Jan Dean

People Love to Push Me

I've been pushed by mums, dads,
sisters, brothers,
grandmas, grandpas,
uncles, aunts,
nieces, nephews,
and even monkeys.

I've been pushed by a poet's pencil,
an artist's paintbrush,
a teacher's red pen,
a drummer's drumstick,
an old pair of scissors,
and the rubbery end of a used toothbrush.

I've been pushed on rainy days in April,
hot days in July,
and snowy days in December.

Most of the time, people push me
without saying a word.
They just stand there
like it's no big deal.
No matter what, though,
I never push them back.

All in all, I love being the buttons in a lift!

Darren Sardelli

What is the World?

A scientist may say:
'70% water, 30% land.'
A geologist may say:
'4.6 billion years old.'
An astronomer may say:
'The merest speck
on a cosmic coast
awash on the tide of time.'
A myth maker may say:
'A glorious orb
held aloft
by elephants
atop a giant turtle.'
A priest may say:
'A miracle.'
An astronaut may say:
'Home.'
An ecologist may say:
'Poorly.'

James Carter

Grief

Grief can catch you
Like fishermen
Catch fish
Caught in a net
By surprise
You're reeled in
Captured
Then sometimes
You're thrown
Back in to the sea
To swim

Debra Bertulis

Playing With Letters and Words

There are many poems that have no rhyme and even have no rhythm, but rely upon their shape, or the way the poem is arranged on the page, to qualify as a poem.

Diamond

O
you
are a
diamond
in the coal
when everyone
is moaning, then
you are the heart
and soul. In you the
stars shine brightly, for
you, even the light will
sing. You gleam and
dream and promise
hope, and so, for
you, my friend
I give this
silver
ring
O

RS

Concrete Poems

In **concrete poems**, or **shape poems**, the words of the poem are arranged in the shape of the poem's subject. In a poem about a dog, for example, the poem would make the shape of a dog on the page.

Calligrams are a type of **concrete poem** in which the letters themselves or the type of printing is used to express visually what the words say. You'll see what I mean when you read my 'Chameleon' poem.

You might think a book of these poems would be very heavy to carry, but luckily concrete poems are not actually made out of concrete!

Hard to Crack

concrete poems
are hard to read
pneumatic
drills
are
what
y
o
u
n
e
e
d
concrete poems are hard to crack
it's builders who have got the knack

John Foster

A Fat Cat

A A
Fat Fat
Cat, Cat,
Licking its furry, black paws,
Stroking its long, straight whiskers,
Washing its triangular, pointed ears,
Soaking up the golden summer sun
That is streaming warmly in
Through the window.
Waiting
For a bird to pass,
For a mouse to scuttle by,
For a spider to emerge from hiding,
For a hand to come and stroke its sleek back,
For someone to come and tickle its soft tummy,
For someone to come and scratch between its ears.
Listening out for the sound of cool milk pouring,
For the sound of the birds in the trees chirping,
For the sound of the dog next door barking,
For the sound of the can opener whirring,
For the sound of the children returning,
For the sound of other cats invading,
For the sound of something moving
In the sleepy summer silence.
Waiting, always waiting
For night to come, and
while it waits it p u r r r r r r r r r r r r s.

Julia Rawlinson

Gales of Laughter

ha ho teehee
ha ho teehee
ha ho teehee
ha ho teehee
ha ho teehee
ha ho teehee
ha ho teehee
ha
ha ho
ha ho
ha ho
hee
teeheehee hee
hee
teeheehee hee
hee
teeheehee hee
hee
teeheehee hee
hee
teeheehee hee
hee
teehee hee
hee
hee
hee
hee

Chrissie Gittins

Chameleon

treetreetreetreetreetreetreetreetreetreetreetreetree
treetreetreetreetreetreetreetreetreetreetreetreetree
treetreetreetreetreetreetreetreetreetreetreetreetree
treetreetreetreetreetreetreetreetreetreetreetreetree
treetreetreetreetreetreetreetreetreetreetreetreetree
treetreetreetreetreetreetreetreetreetreetreetreetree
treetreetreetreetreetreetreetreetreetreetreetreetree
treetreetreetreetreetreetreetreetreetreetreetreetree
treetreetreetreetreetreetreetreetreetreetreetreetree
treetreetreetreetreetreetreetreetreetree**you**tree**can**tree
searchtree**all**tree**day**treetreetreeetreeetreetre**but**tree
you'lltree**never**tree**see**treetreetreetreetreetreetree
treetreetreetreetreetreetreetreetreetreetreetreetree
treetreetreetrreetreetreetreetreetreetreethetreetreetree
treetreetreetreetreetretreetreetreetreetreetreetreetree
treereetreetreetreetreetreetreetreetreetreetreetreetree
treetreetreetreetreetreetreetreetreetreetreetreetree
thetreetreetreetreetreetreetreetreetreetreechameleontree
treeeetreetreetreetreetreetreetreetreetreetreetreetree**hiding**
treetreetreetreetreetreetreetretreetreetreetreetreetree
treetreetreetreetreetreetreetreetreetreetreetreetree
treetretreetreetreetreetreetreetreetreetree**in**treetree**the**tree
treetreetreetreetreetreetreetreetretreetreetreetreetree
treetreetreetreetreetreetreetreetreetreetreetreetreetre
treetreetreetreetreetreetreetreetreetreetreetreetree
treetreetreetreetreetreetreetreetreetretreetreetreetree
treetreetreetreetreetreetreetreetreetreetreetreetree
treetreetreetretree**tree**treetreetreetreetreetreetreetree

RS

Acrostics and Their Friends

An **acrostic** is a piece of writing in which the first letter, syllable or word of each line spells out a word or a message. An **acrostic** can be used as a mnemonic device – that means an aid to help you remember something. For example, the phrase Richard Of York Gave Battle In Vain is a way in which we remember the order of the colours of the rainbow (red, orange, yellow, green, blue indigo, violet). **Acrostics** can also be used in puzzles.

There are lots of different ways to write an **acrostic**. In my 'Happy and Sad' poem I have made the last letter of each line of the second verse spell the word SAD, in contrast to the first verse, where I have used the first letters to spell HAPPY.

Happy and Sad

Hugs
Apples
Playtime
Pets
Yellow

jes**S**
dropped her pizz**A**
and crie**D**

RS

But **acrostics** have friends. There are **double acrostics,** where each line begins and ends in the letters of the chosen word. **Mesostics** have the word running down the middle of the poem. You may even spot a very rare **horizontic**, where the poem is written in a single line, but the important letters are picked out in capitals.

These may be complicated-sounding titles, but the poems are great fun – to read and to write. See if you can find the hidden words in these poems.

Rabbit Run

Beneath the hedgerows,
Under the trees, we
Run for cover in one of these.
Rooks call out when the sly
Old fox is about.
We listen and
Stiffen like rocks. Then run.

Jill Townsend

8

Amid the cluttered corner of a living room,
Resting in the shadow of a sofa cushion,
A miniature monster waits to perform as
Carnival stilt walker, cloaked in dark horror.
His eight eyes focus, his eight legs tense.
Nobody can predict his path, or his intention.
Icy fear spreads and grips as you notice the
Deliberate flexing of legs. Can you feel the phobia?

Coral Rumble

A Sunny Day

what a way to Start the day
with hUmming bees
a cricket siNging
the chit chat of birdS in the tree
we are Happy
the cold is fleeIng the afternoon
and you preseNt us with a sky
of apricot, pEach and gold

RS

Class Four Third Prize
Second To None

The Barrage of applause
The envy of my cLassmates
Universal acclamation
The Sheer approval
The long walk to the front of tHe assembly
First time I'd won anything in my life
The experieNce
Third prize in the handwritinG competition 1978

Ian Bland

Horizon

Such coloUrs iN the distant Sky Evoking mysTery

RS

Rescue

hOpe or a mirAge, Shimmering In the deSert?

RS

Ox-writing

The lines in this type of poem do just what a tractor does when it is ploughing a field. First it goes up the field, then it goes down the field. This is an example of **boustrophedon**, or **ox-writing**, where the lines reverse direction. You have to read one line left to right and the next line right to left for the words to make sense. These types of poem are called **ox-writing** because before tractors were invented it was oxen who pulled ploughs up and down the fields.

Tractor

Dressed in a coat of mud
soil with splattered and
the farm tractor coughs and rasps
.throat bad a with horn factory a like

Huge tyres heave
field soggy the through plough the
churning the dark earth into
.waves frozen like shapes

Seagulls swoop and glide behind
free flowing ribbons wild like
in some great wind.

up and down ,down and Up
the valley all day long

pierce lights its evening By
the gathering dusk
fields the over rolls growl its and
like a tumbling echo.

night star-filled the Slowly
covers the countryside in a warm dark
.Plough silent own its brings that

John Rice

Words Within Words

These are both poems and puzzles. Inside the words of the poem, smaller words can be found hiding.

A Beggar Eats a Boiled Egg

a beggar eats
a boiled egg

half a bagel
from a bag

on a street
without a tree

her cage
is age

she knows
now

a beetle
from a bee

she holds
her old

life
as if

a shell
she were

in search
of sea

Steve Withrow

Finding What's Fishy in Fortunate

Search for what's false in believing,
look for damage in the pharmacy,
in the garage you'll find anger,
in the cupboard there's a wild beast hiding
and there's a little bit of evil in messiness.

But, looking on the bright side,
the garbageman's holding a jewel,
there's something jolly in the funeral,
there's romance in being slovenly,
much joy in cancelations
and a great big smile in the grinder.

Trevor Parsons

Anagram Poems

If you know what an **anagram** is, then you'll know what these poems do – they take the subject of the poem and mix up the letters to make new words.

Mosquito

Oi
Mosi

Quit,
Mosi,
Quit!

RS

Not Just Words

Poets can have fun with numbers too.

I One-der What Two Do?

I 1der what 2 do 2day.
Something just 4 fun.
I don't want 2 play 10is
4 I have never 1.

2day I'm feeling lazy,
I shall get up L8,
take the K9 4 a walk
and go and find my m8s.

Holidays are 3 and easy,
it's gr8 2 be alive!
2morrow we go back 2 school.
How will I sur5?

Jane Clarke

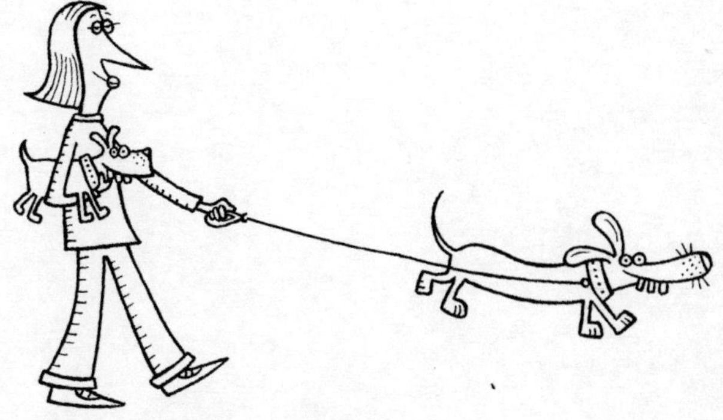

Sorting the Syllables, Letters and Lines

Many forms of poetry rely on the number of lines in the poem, or the number of words, or the number of syllables. Poems that rely on a particular rhythm, such as **blank verse**, have their syllables arranged according to how much emphasis, or stress, you place on a word when you say it.

In **blank verse**, when you read it aloud, you can clearly hear the di **dum** di **dum** di **dum** di **dum** di **dum** rhythm. (Shakespeare's plays are mostly written in blank verse.)

Many rhyming poems rely on a rhythm too, from **limericks** to **sonnets**. But we are going to look at some of the less-rhythmic and non-rhyming poems that rely on counting for their form.

One-word Poems

Some people might say that these are not really poems. But I think they qualify. What do you think? They are meant to be fun. The clever bit is in the title, which can be as long as you like. For example:

A One-word Poem That Can Make A Room Full of Small Children Laugh

Bottom

Joshua Seigal

Haiku

Haiku is a form of Japanese poetry. They consist entirely of 17 syllables, written in three lines containing 5, 7 and 5 syllables respectively. A **haiku** should be said in one breath. Traditionally, it should always be about nature. And it should, strictly, mention one of the seasons – spring, summer, autumn or winter. But these days many poets don't stick to that rule. A **haiku** shouldn't have a title, though that's another rule that often gets broken.

Echoing around
the small cave of this conch shell
an entire ocean

Graham Denton

Castles in the sky
Darken in the winter wind
And then the rain comes

Jill Pryor

Having said that **haiku** must be written in three lines of 5, 7 and 5 syllables, I am now going to confuse you by adding that this is not always the case. The Japanese language is not like English; instead of using letters, it is written in symbols, or characters. For example: カタカナ or 片仮名.

So many famous Japanese **haiku**, when translated into English, end up with a different number of syllables. Poets writing in English and other languages that use the same alphabet as us sometimes vary the number. Here is a haiku written with 3, 4 and 3 syllables.

heron spears –
the fish swims on
in the air

Liz Brownlee

Senryu

Senryu are similar to **haiku** but they are written about people rather than nature. **Senryu** can be serious, but are usually comic, like these examples. The last one says it is a haiku, but of course it's not, it's a senryu! And it breaks the 'no title' rule. Which just goes to show that you can do what you want with poetry, really...

Look at you in that
daft three-cornered pirate hat!
Can I have it please?

RS

Knocked-off Haiku

Knock a haiku off
his baiku and he'll ride on
but he won't laiku

Rupert Smith

Tanka

Tanka are similar to **haiku**, but written in five lines of 5, 7, 5, 7 and 7 syllables. As with **haiku** the syllable count will sometimes be fewer. The important thing is to have a short line, then a longer one, another short one and then two longer lines.

The third line of a tanka is very important. It is often described as **pivotal**. It should refer back to lines one and two, and forward to four and five. You can see how this works if you read the following **tanka** as two joined-together **haiku**. The third line is the last line of the first **haiku**, but is also the first line of the second.

Sally has my pen
Billy Smith gave it to her
Give me back my pen!
Billy said it was his pen.
Will he want his football back?

RS

a praying mantis
sunbathes on the hot canvas
this is exciting
crickets zing in the brown grass
alarm is set for midnight

RS

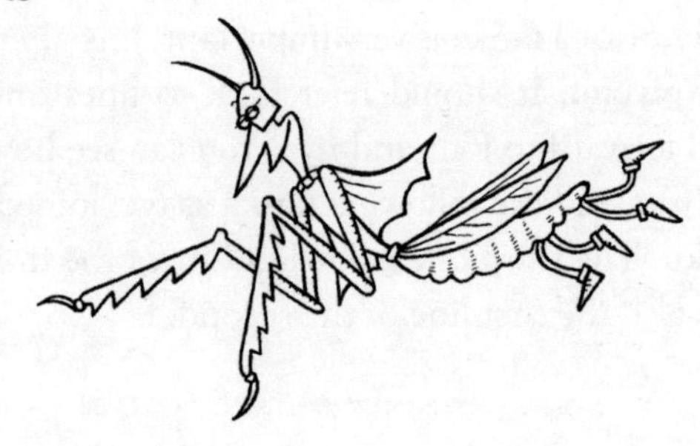

a pigeon glides by
on a gentle sigh of wind
I marvel
Superman flies through the sky
A million pounds of CGI

RS

Cinquains

Cinquains were invented by the American poet Adelaide Crapsey who lived over a hundred years ago. They have five lines of 2, 4, 6, 8 and 2 syllables.

November Night

Listen ...
With faint dry sound,
Like steps of passing ghosts,
The leaves, frost-crisp'd, break from the trees
And fall.

Adelaide Crapsey

Tea for Two

tea pot
Grannie is 'mum'
she lives all alone now
Grandad drank it from a saucer
she says

RS

Sewing Accident

gran's purse
has a hole in
so she mends it with thread
now she has a pound coin in the
lining

RS

My Dog

Jasper
fluffy cotton
timid dog runs away
scraping chairs and he runs upstairs
to hide

Sam Decie (aged 7)

Univocalic

Here's another complicated-sounding type of poem that can be great fun to write. A **univocalic** is a poem that uses only a single vowel A, E, I, O, or U, and no others.

Newts

They've keen eyes,
wee needle teeth,
Newts seek teeny prey.

The very few weeks
when fevered newts breed
they need the wet.

When we see newts,
even newts' eggs,
let's let them be.

Philip Waddell

Deer Reed

Three deer tremble by the September elms
where scree defends tree.
Reeds jerk where the creek ebbs.

Here the kestrel queen preens herself:
she reflects the fever screech event –
the resentment sphere –
never seeks her sweet shell eye-sleep.

John Rice

Box of Frogs

Spotty frogs, dotty frogs
Lots of grotty frogs
Hot, old hoppy frogs
Oh so stroppy frogs.
Odd frogs, potty frogs
Lots of snotty frogs
Bold, old floppy frogs
Oh so soppy frogs.
Lots of frogs
Hop, hop, hop.
No, bold, old frogs,
Don't stop, don't stop

Celia Warren

Pick a Letter

As I've said before, poets love to have fun with letters and words. Here is a poem that celebrates a letter that is never heard.

The Silent H

We are the honest Hs
You will find us in each hour.
We present Rhona with rhinestones
And give heirlooms to heirs
We play rhapsodies on Rhodes
Grow rhubarb on the Rhine
And look after rhinos.
We've got rhythm
We can find you a rhyme.
We are the honest Hs.

John Foster

Kennings

Kennings began life in Scandinavia and are associated with Old Norse (ancient Norwegian), Icelandic and Anglo-Saxon poetry. A single word, such as 'sword', is replaced by two words that describe the object, but in a more interesting way. So 'sword' might become 'iron wounder'.

Goalie

Ace defender
Ball plucker
Muddy scrambler
Fast diver
Crowd sorter
Ball puncher
Long kicker
Expert thrower
Ball catcher
Time passer
Wall builder
Goal saver
Game winner

RS

My Mum

Waker upper
Cuddle maker
Sadness breaker
Good cooker
Nice looker
Read booker
Groovy dancer
Joke laugher
Love giver
Clothes sorter
Holiday bringer
Outing planner
Garden planter
School driver
Tucker inner
Night nighter

Jill Pryor

Alphabet Poems

I probably don't need to explain what **alphabet poems** are; as you can see, every line has to start with each letter of the alphabet in order. But the alphabet doesn't always have to start and finish at the beginning and end, and sometimes poets choose to make individual words rather than the lines start with each letter!

London

Zealous young xylophonists wait vacantly
under thundery skies,
rarely quiet,
playing on,
nightly.

Melodies lurk knowingly,
jingle, invade hearts,
glide from each deep corner,
begging answers.

Judith Nicholls

A to Z

A up said me dad,
B off to bed with you.
C it's half past eight and I've
Decided that from now on it's bed before nine.
E can't be serious I thought.
F he carries on like this I'll never see any TV
G I'll lose my grasp of American slang.
H not fair.
I won't go.
J think I should protest?
K I will.
L O said me dad,
M not standing for this
N y kid thinks he can disobey me has got another
think coming.
O yes he has!
P then wash your hands and face, do your teeth and
straight to bed.
Q then, your sister will have finished soon.
R you ready yet? Wash that face properly
S pecially round your nose It's disgusting.
T? No you can't. If you drink tea now you will wet
the bed
U will you know.
V end of a perfect day. Now I'll tuck you in.

W you up – to save space. Then I can fit your brother
in too – and the dog and the hamster. There you all fit in
Xactly
Y don't you like it? It's cosy, space saving, economical.
Go to sleep. Not a peep. Do exactly as I
Z ZZZZZZZZZZZZZZZZZZZZzz

Michaela Morgan

Edible Alphabet!

Eat five greasy hippos in juicy ketchup? Lovely!
Munch nine oily partridges quite rapidly? Superb!
Taste underdone vulture with eggs? Yum!
Zebra… anything but…
Crocodile dung!

Andrea Shavick

Prose Poetry

A **prose poem** is a curious thing. It tells a short story. But it's more than a story because it uses lots of poetic tricks, such as rhythm, similes, alliteration and internal rhyme. It's often written like a story rather than in verses, stanzas and lines, so it doesn't look like a poem, but it has to be poetic. Some people say that it's neither poetry nor prose so needs to be in a category all of its own.

Clarinet Lesson

I am walking home, after my clarinet lesson and anticipating supper, humming a tune that was a big hit for Acker Bilk in nineteen sixty-two called Stranger on the Shore. I open the door to my first-floor flat. There is a snake on the stairs. A hissing, hooded cobra rears ready to strike. Luckily I have my clarinet with me.

RS

How to Create a Chinese Dragon

Start with the body of a serpent, weld on the horns of a stag – a fitting crown for an emperor. Set in the dark jewels of rabbits' eyes and manicure the dragon's nails so it has the claws of a tiger. Decorate all over with the silvery scales of a carp, a barbel and a pike. With firm needlework, fasten on the leathery ears of the bull. Breathe life into your creation when full of wisdom and passion. The marvellous tail twitches and shudders as life travels down its length. You have made a creature who can row on land, fly on sea and swim through air. It is the one, the many, the immortal.

Angela Topping

Can These Really Be Poems?

People have been arguing for years about whether certain types of rhymes and other writing can be called poetry. Sometimes the content of a poem, what the poem is really about, is more important than what it looks like, or how it's put together. You have to decide what you think is poetry, or poetic...

Chants

Football chants rhyme, and have a rhythm, and are often sung to the tune of well-known songs. But are they poetry? I think good ones probably are. Bad ones probably aren't.

Billy Smith

2 – 4 – 6 – 8
Who do we appreciate?
B – I – L – L – Y
What's that spell?
BILLY!
S – M – I – T – H
What's that spell?

SMITH!
Grove Park Junior is our name
and Billy Smith has WON THE GAME!

RS

Fara Williams Forever

Fara Williams is her name,
Lionesses rule!
In extra-time, we won the game,
Lionesses rule!
With a spot-kick here, a spot-kick there,
here a kick, there a kick,
everywhere a spot-kick.
Fara Williams is her name,
Lionesses rule!

Thanks to Fara's penalty:
Lionesses rule!
England's beaten Germany:
Lionesses rule!
With a spot-kick here, a spot-kick there,
here a kick, there a kick,
everywhere a spot-kick.
Thanks to Fara's penalty:
Lionesses rule!

World Cup Women won third place:
Lionesses rule!
The biggest smile on every face:
Lionesses rule!
With a spot-kick here, a spot-kick there,
here a kick, there a kick,
everywhere a spot-kick.
World Cup Women won third place:
Lionesses rule!

Doggerel and Cliché

Doggerel is a word that describes something that looks like a poem, but is just not very good or very well written. It usually rhymes and it has a rhythm, but the ideas are rarely original. It often uses really obvious rhymes (like 'moon' and 'June') and repeats obvious **similes** and **metaphors** and **clichés** (like 'fluffy clouds of cotton wool') that have been used hundreds of times before.
You can find **clichés** everywhere, of course, not just in **doggerel** – people sometimes even talk in **clichés** – but they are often found in poorly written poems.

The Poetry Cliché Prize

When I walked on to the stage
I felt like the cat that got the cream
Every dog has its day
Then I woke up
And found it was only a dream

RS

Scotsman **William McGonagall** wrote such awful verse that he has become famous for doggerel. His work is so clumsy it is often unintentionally humorous. I think he believed he was a great poet. He is now famous for being a really bad one!

The Tay Bridge Disaster

It must have been an awful sight,
To witness in the dusky moonlight,
While the Storm Fiend did laugh, and angry did bray,
Along the Railway Bridge of the Silv'ry Tay,
Oh! ill-fated Bridge of the Silv'ry Tay,
I must now conclude my lay
By telling the world fearlessly without the least dismay,
That your central girders would not have given way,
At least many sensible men do say,
Had they been supported on each side with buttresses,
At least many sensible men confesses,
For the stronger we our houses do build,
The less chance we have of being killed.

William McGonagall

Although there have been some great lyrics written for pop and rock songs, sadly the words are often **doggerel**. Sometimes, if the music is really good, this doesn't matter. But when you're writing a poem it does matter. So don't write doggerel and avoid clichés like the plague!

Even though this poem calls itself doggerel, it isn't. It's just playing with the word.

Doggerel

Caterwaul, Cockerel
Mackerel, Doggerel
I have cooked some words for you.

Doggerel, Cockerel
Mackerel, Caterwaul
Come and taste a phrase or two.

Cockerel, Caterwaul
Doggerel, Mackerel
Eat them up, and if you flag…

Mackerel, Doggerel
Caterwaul, Cockerel
You shall have a doggerel bag.

Mike Barfield

Nursery Rhymes

Most people's first experience of poems comes in the form of **nursery rhymes** – the **lullabies**, counting games, **riddles** and rhymed **fables** that introduce us to the rhythmic, mnemonic, allegorical uses of language in songs sung to us by our mothers and fathers, grandmothers and grandfathers.

Did you know that some nursery rhymes have been around for hundreds of years and have a meaning that most of us have forgotten?

Humpty Dumpty sat on the wall

Humpty Dumpty had a great fall

All the King's horses and all the King's men

Couldn't put Humpty together again!

Humpty Dumpty actually existed. But he wasn't an egg. Nor was he a person. Humpty Dumpty was in fact a cannon belonging to supporters of King Charles I in the English Civil War. He sat on a church tower in Colchester until an enemy barrage destroyed the tower and he fell to the ground below, where he broke into several pieces.

For the episode when Alice meets Humpty Dumpty in Lewis Carroll's **Alice Through the Looking Glass,** the illustrator decided to turn the cannon into an egg. (No one knows why.) The book was hugely popular and so a generation of children grew up thinking Humpty Dumpty was a nonsense rhyme about an egg.

Ring a ring a roses,
A pocket full of posies

A-tish-oo, a-tish-oo

We all fall down

Now, most people think this nursery rhyme does have another meaning and that it's to do with the Black Death. But it was written five hundred years after the Plague, and in the original version there's no mention of sneezing. So this probably really is just a nonsense verse, which was used in a children's game.

I enjoy writing new versions of nursery rhymes. It's good fun. Why don't you try it?

Little Miss Muffet

Little Miss Muffet
Sat down on a tuffet
Eating her well-balanced diet
There came a big spider
And sat down beside her
Very politely and quiet

RS

Mary Had a Little Lamp-post

Mary had a little lamp-post
Its light was very bright
And everywhere that Mary went
The lamp-post just sat tight

It wouldn't go to school with her
And this made her see red
So she chopped it down with an axe she'd found
And took a lamb instead

RS and Michael Leigh

Riddles

Can riddles and puzzles also be poems? Lots of riddles have been handed down to us by word of mouth, like nursery rhymes. They are composed with a rhythm and rhyme to help people remember them. And many are written in a poetic form. But are they poems? Again, I'll let you decide. See if you can solve these. The answers are in a poem of their own...

The Fifth?

The beginning of eternity
The end of time and space
The beginning of every end
And the end of every place

Anon

Flower

What always runs
but never walks,
often murmurs,
never talks,
has a bed
but never sleeps,
has a mouth
but never eats?

Anon

A Riddle

There is one that has a head without an eye,
And there's one that has an eye without a head.
You may find the answer if you try;
And when all is said,
Half the answer hangs upon a thread.

Christina Rossetti

Crumbs

My first is in baker and also in bread
My second's in miller and also in bread
My third is in cake and also in bread
My fourth is in wrapper and also in bread
My last is in doughnut and also in bread

My whole thing is found
Near the mouth, more or less,
And you often find crumbs there.
What am I? Can you guess?

RS

Riddle

It trickles on many soft,
hooked feet,
tethered by shape
and appetite,
tirelessly lacing leafy spreads
until its hunger empties
into a silk-held pool
mid-worlds;
it emerges
stretching soft,
damp wings,
to find its form
from air and flight,
sip and escape
the secret vessels
of the flowers
and taste the sky.

Liz Brownlee

Answers

E is fifth in the ABC
A **river** flows downstream
Eye of a **needle**, a **pin** has a head
A **beard** catches crumbs
A cocoon is a **damselfly**'s bed

RS

Having a Laugh

Although writing poems can be hard work, poets don't always take themselves too seriously. Great poems don't have to be terribly serious. They can be clever without using long, complicated words. Good poetry is often funny. In this section you'll find adverts in verse, poems about poems, poems made by cutting up magazines, poems that are copies of other poems and just plain old-fashioned nonsense.

Adverts

You can have great fun writing **adverts** for things. Here you can buy a drum kit, find a girlfriend (as long as you enjoy swimming and have a tail) and pick up some poetry bargains. But there's more to these adverts than first meets the eye, which is why I think they qualify as poems.

Drum Kit For Sale

Drum Kit For Sale
Guaranteed to make house shake
Very Loud Indeed
(Gave Mum a headache.)

Drum Kit For Sale
Snappy snare – terrific tone
Dad says – Must go at any price!

(Or will exchange
for trombone.)

RS

Lonely Heart

Long-necked lake monster
1500 years old
(but look a lot younger)
would like to meet similar
water-loving creature
to share murky depths
in Scottish Highlands.
Enjoys swims,
nocturnal wanderings,
fish suppers,
and the natural world.
Dislikes include
boat cruises,
sonar scans,
and flashing
tourists' cameras.
Interested?
Then please drop me a line
to this address:
Loch Ness

Graham Denton

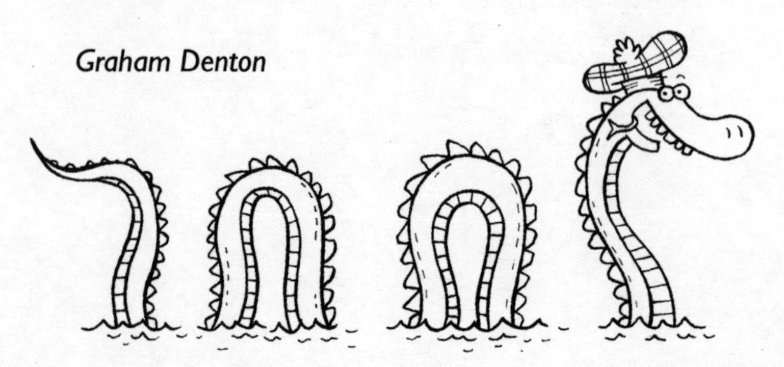

Poetry Shop Closing Down: All Stock Must Go

Haiku – in a bin
at the bottom of the aisle
next to the sonnets.

Limericks have had their day
It's clear they've got nothing to say
Some find them rude
Vulgar and crude
They're free if you'll take them away

Free Verse is draped all over the shop.
Although it's free
there is a modest charge
for each clump of words.

Cinquains
are down aisle five.
You can hear them counting
their syllables. Eight in this line.
Buy two?

Bernard Young

Poems About Poems

Poets love playing around with the idea of poetry. These poems ask questions, talk about themselves and can be quite badly behaved.

Party Poem

We poems are often thought to be
quiet, serious, boring, even sad
and sometimes we are.

But poems can be fun too!
Take me – I love nothing better
than a lively get-together

which is why the editor
has especially invited me
to join the others in this anthology.

So don't just sit there, come on in,
grab a poem, shake an elegy…
Let's have a poetry party!

Philip Waddell

A Poem Is A Fragile Thing

A poem
is a fragile,
fluttering thing
emerging slowly
as a creature
of wet wings
and possibilities.
A poem knows
without the help
of prodding,
impatient fingers
the how
and the when.
Yet,
even now,
I find the wing dust
of this poem
on my hands
and know
I have held it
too long.

Eric Ode

Cut-ups and Collage

William Carlos Williams is one of my favourite poets. He wrote a poem called 'The Locust Tree in Flower', which consists of thirteen lines. But on each line there is only word. I made my version of this type of poem by writing down, on a large sheet of paper, as many words and phrases about September that I could think of. Then I cut them out and rearranged them to make a poem.

September

After William Carlos Williams

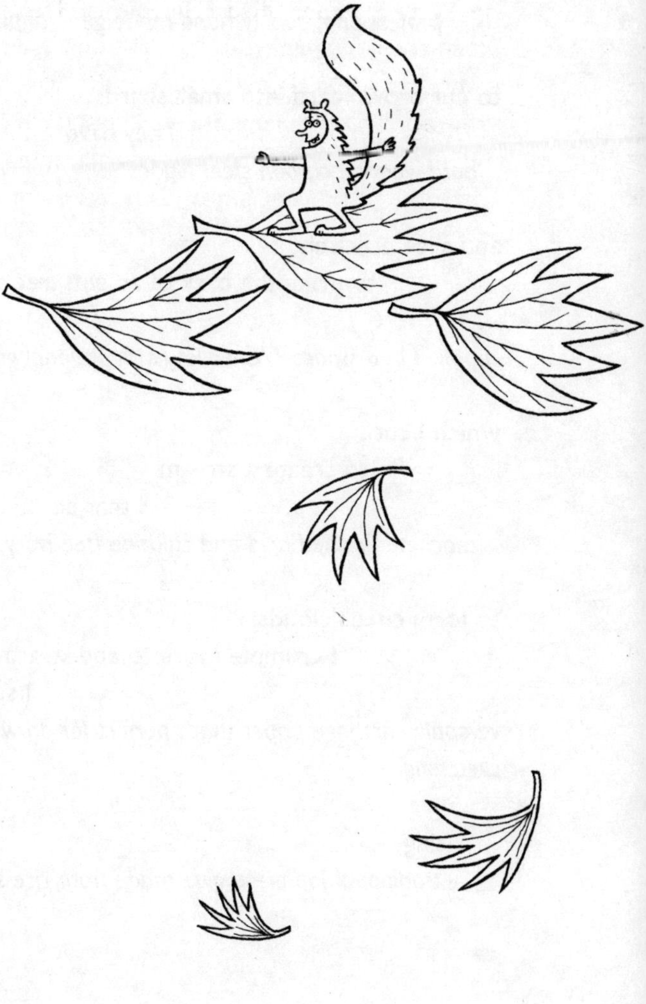

leaf
fall
gold

wet
rake
deck

chair
conkers
rolled

beach
ball
gets

burst
scars
cold

ache
first
frost

RS

Collage

I use my
professional quality hand-made general purpose scissors

to cut brown card into small shards.
They have
hard-wearing carbon steel blades

and slice precisely
to make the bark of an elm tree.
They are
supplied in a smart PVC wallet (with optional gift box available)

which I cut
to create a stream.
I tear some
machine finished acid and chlorine free ivory tissue paper

to form cirrus clouds.
I crumple more to add stratocumulus.
I stick this to
versatile cartridge paper that's perfect for drawing and sketching

using
traditional Japanese glue made from rice starch.

I give it to Dad, who puts it in
a 120 gauge thick black sack, ideal for light duty uses

and tells me
to do something useful
for once.

Laura Mucha

Ten Torn Messages

Found on Shelf	*Found in Bin*
window cleaner is under the doormat	Money for
walking Dinner is in the oven	Dog needs
Bill is behind the clock	Electricity
dustbin – expecting Granny soon!	Please put rubbish in
fridge – needs warming!	Baby's bottle in
the windows love Fred	Please close
sausages Please fetch washing in	Have bought some
the dentist can't stop	Am on my way to
the dotted line Will see you at 5pm	Please sign on
forget to close the gate	Dog gone missing You always

Celia Warren

Of course, you don't have to write poetry on the computer, or even on paper...

Leaves

In the midst of today's bluster
I collected four
Of the dry autumn leaves
That had settled in my garden.
On each one, in indelible pen,
I wrote a single word of my sentence
Then returned them to their roost.

I have told you what I have done,
But you will never know what
I gave back to the wind.

John H. Rice

New Poems From Old

Are poems that copy other poems really poems? Well, of course they are. Poets have been writing parodies of poems since the beginning of verse, when ballads were passed on by word of mouth. Sometimes to make fun of the poet who wrote the original, sometimes just for laughs and sometimes as a tribute, because the original was so good other poets wanted to try their skill at emulating it.

But if you base your poem on one that another poet has written, the usual thing to do is to credit the original. Poets usually write something like 'in the style of...' or 'after...' – as I did with my 'September' poem.

One of the most copied poems ever must be Kit Wright's wonderful 'Magic Box'. Here's Joshua Seigal's version:

The Nasty Box

(after Kit Wright)

I will put in the box

the bark of a dog, keeping me awake at night,
the graze on my knee from when I fell over,
lava from the mouth of a vicious volcano.

I will put in the box

a snowball filled with bits of dirt,
a fizzy drink that's gone warm and flat,
a stomach ache and a trip to the doctor.

I will put into the box

the deafening taunts of a thousand bullies,
a snarling teacher with sharpened fangs
and the angry red crosses on my failed homework.

I will put into the box

the time my brother told on me,
a burglar stealing a wedding ring
and a footballer with a broken leg.

My box is fashioned from decaying bark
with fungus on the lid and disappointment in the
corners.

Its hinges are the knuckles of terrible ogres.

I shall bury my box
deep in the bowels of a dense forest
where, like a lost tribe,
it will never be discovered.

Joshua Seigal

Little Miss Muffet

Little Miss Muffet
Sat on a tuffet
Eating her curds and whey
There came a huge, green and loathsome monster
with a drooling mouth, dripping saliva
and sharp, yellow, jagged teeth
and hairy hands with long, dirty, curling fingernails
And Miss Muffet said,
What happened to the spider?

RS

Nonsense Verse

I've always loved nonsense verse. When I was young my favourite book was *Alice in Wonderland*, which is full of 'stuff and nonsense' as Alice herself says. The important thing about nonsense verse is, of course, that it has to make its own kind of sense. Er... does that make sense?

One bright morning in the middle of the night,
Two dead boys got up to fight.
Back-to-back they faced one another,
Drew their swords and shot each other.
One was blind and the other couldn't see,
So they chose a dummy for a referee.
A blind man went to see fair play,
A dumb man went to shout 'hooray!'
A deaf policeman heard the noise,
And came and killed those two dead boys.
A paralysed donkey walking by,
Kicked the copper in the eye,
Sent him through a rubber wall,
Into a dry ditch and drowned them all.
(If you don't believe this lie is true,
Ask the blind man – he saw it too!)

Anon

Lesser Known Children's Games

Scribble Scrobble
Tease the Tiger
Throw the Worm Over the Wall
Shout Monkey!
Who's Hidden Harriet?
How Far Can You Fall?

Hop Irish.
Skip Welsh.
Jump Over the Moat
Chase the Goldfish
Hurl the Spoon
Put the Coat on the Stoat

Last One Up the Chimney is a Sooty Beggar
Turnip Ball
Kiss the Rat
Snakes and Larders
Pancake Frisbee
Put the Hat on the Spratt

RS

Gherkin Car

I am the Picasso of Poetry
Ear nose blue pink eye spoon
Burnt ochre
Sienna
Five plums a tenner
A six-year-old child could write this
Exclamation mark
Wonky donkey
Bob

RS

And Finally...

This last section contains some poems that don't rhyme, but have a structure and rhythm, free verse and a few odds and ends that didn't really fit in anywhere else in the book but that I'd like to share with you.

Instead

Instead of an XBox
please show me a pathway that stretches to the stars.
Instead of a mobile phone
please teach me the language I need to help me speak
  with angels.
Instead of a computer
please reveal to me the mathematics of meteors
  and motion.
Instead of the latest computer game
please come with me on a search for dragons in the
  wood behind our house.
Instead of an e-reader
please read to me from a book of ancient knowledge.
Instead of a digital camera
please help me remember faces and places, mystery
  and moonbeams.
Instead of a 3-D TV
please take me to an empty world that I can people
  with my imagination.
Instead of electronic wizardry
please show me how to navigate the wisdom
  inside of me.

Brian Moses

Free Verse

Free verse has the cadence, or natural rhythm, of spoken language, and delights in not having any obvious form or style, other than being written in short lines to distinguish it from prose.

I Am a Free Verse Poem

I am a free verse poem.
I am not shackled
by the constraints of form.
My words can wander across the page
without having to worry
about the number of syllables per line
or the need to rhyme.
If I feel like it,
up
I can go and
down,
sdrawkcab and forwards.
There are no boundaries confusing me,
no set of rules that I must follow.
I am happier than a haiku.
The song I sing is my own.
I can pattern the page
however I like.
I am a free verse poem.

John Foster

Waiting for Dolphins

The strong breeze buffeted my face and I shivered.
The crowd with their cameras fanned the shore;
anticipating and expecting.
Some sat on the wet sand; others stood up.
We waited for the North Sea dolphins to leap and
feast on the sardine shoal.
But the dolphins took their time.

The crunch, crunch of the crushed pebbles under our
feet;
The low tide left crabs and clams to be scavenged by
hungry seagulls and curlews.
Waiting and waiting were children skimming stones in
the water.
We lingered so long for this weekly nature show.
But the dolphins took their time.

The grey sand, the grey sea and the grey sky
sandwiched our view; making the scene like some
bleak photograph.
The crowd grew and stretched on the sandy shore.
People with thick coats, gloved hands nursed their
cup of early morning tea.
But the dolphins took their time.

Then, suddenly, a squeal of delight; a movement arose
in the right.
In the corner of my eye, I saw them, what we have
been longing to see.
They dove in beautiful succession.
Everyone, young and old, clapped together.
For the dolphins had finally come.

Rita Antoinette Borg

This may not strictly be a poem, but it's written by a very good writer and it's an interesting way to play with words. You may not know what sarsaparilla is, or have ever eaten apple halves spread with peanut butter – but that's because you're not American like this poet.

Word Games

Finding small words inside bigger words was the way my mother tried to get us to sleep at night. She'd make us apple halves with peanut butter and bring them to our bedroom on a plate, raisins stuck in for the eyes and nose, and a slice of carrot cut in the shape of a half moon for the mouth.

In the month of September all her long words began with an 's': *silliness, sarsaparilla* and *summertime*. From those I made *lines* and *pairs* and *timers*.

In October she chose *octopus, oration* and *ochre*. I thought of pouts and rant and oh. My mother said two-letter words didn't count.

November brought *naughtiness, nothing* and *Neverland* and I came up with *night, toning* and *Denver*. My mother said we weren't allowed place names.

Now it's December and my mother's given us *darkness, dreariness* and *depressed* because she says she hates the winter. I changed those into *dress, readiness* and *presents* because I was thinking of Christmas.

Mum said there isn't an 'n' or a 't' in *depressed* but she would let us have presents anyway.

Cheryl Moskowitz

Part 2: How to Write Brilliant Poetry

Writing poems is much easier than most people think. In fact, if you've ever written a poem you'll know this is true. All you have to do is follow a few simple rules and you'll have a poem. If you become good at it you can even make up a few rules of your own.

Of course, writing *brilliant* poetry is more difficult. I can explain what you need to do but I'm afraid I can't guarantee that your poem will be brilliant. I can't even guarantee that my own poems will be brilliant. What I can say is that writing poetry is brilliant fun.

In this part of the book I'll tell you how to write **cinquains, mesostics, advert poems** and **cut-up poems** and give you a list of all the things I've found useful when writing poetry, from when I very first started about a hundred years ago right up to tomorrow!

Write It Down

Number one on that list is KEEP A NOTEBOOK. This is very important. I always carry a notebook around with me, everywhere I go. You never know when you're going to get a good idea for a poem, do you? Or a good idea for something else, for that matter.

I take my notebook to bed with me. Before you go to sleep or first thing in the morning are both good times for thinking of something you can turn into a poem. And have you ever woken up in the night with a good idea? I bet you have. Well, if you've got your notebook by the bed you can write it down. If you don't write it down, you'll probably have forgotten it by the morning.

Write anything and everything you think of in your notebook. You may never use some of your ideas, or some of the lines or rhymes you quickly scribble in there. But that doesn't matter. You don't have to show anyone else your notebook. It is just for you. And when you sit down to write a poem, you'll have it there to remind you of all the ideas you've had.

Most people think that you have to be super talented to write poems or that you need a fantastic imagination. Well, the best poets are very talented, but they usually have to work quite hard to make their poems as good as they are. And even the most brilliant poets in the world had to start somewhere.

Be Imaginative

Using your imagination comes with practice. Everyone has an imagination, it's just that some people, usually grown-ups, forget they do. I meet lots of children with fantastic imaginations, who have lots of ideas and stories in their heads, and lots of grown-ups who say they can't think of anything to write about. They can really, it's just that growing up got in the way a bit and they forgot. And, like anything, practice is important. So if you never use your imagination, it might forget how to work, but use it lots and you'll find you have ideas aplenty.

Start Here

Usually, if you're having trouble thinking of something, you just need a starting point. But if you follow the advice in the next few sections, you should find that your imagination will start to get going. And remember, not all ideas are going to be good ideas. But all of them matter. Write them all down in your notebook. You can sort out the good from the not so good later.

Cinquains

Cinquains are very similar to **haiku** and **tanka** poems. They are short, with just five lines (from the French *cinq*, which means five) and each line has to have an exact number of syllables. They were invented by the American poet Adelaide Crapsey about a hundred years ago. The great thing about them is that they are easy to write. Here's what we have to do.

Line one has two syllables, so let's start by thinking about the **subject** of our poem. What shall we write about? How about choosing an animal? You could choose a tiger or giraffe (they both have two syllables) or you could maybe think of a more unusual animal. How about an aardvark or an ostrich? Or you could write about a pet or a domestic animal. A chicken would make a good subject I think. I asked my grandson Sam to help me write this, and he decided to write a poem about a spider.

Line two has four syllables, and **describes** the spider. Sam chose *Teenie weenie.* That describes a spider well I think. A very small spider, anyway. He could have made the spider really big. But *Real-ly big* has only three syllables, so you would have to add another syllable, for example, *She's really big.*) Or you could use *It's venomous.* Or *Very hairy*. Try lots of possibilities until you find the one you like the best.

Line three has six syllables. It's an **action** line. The spider in your poem needs to be doing something. Sam chose *Spinning amazing webs.*

Line four has eight syllables. In this line we think

about the poem, and what we're writing about, **how it makes us feel**. It's a chance to add a little emotion to the poem. How do you feel about the spider, or about spiders generally? Or maybe you can tell us how the spider feels about you. Sam described how he himself felt, and used a simile. He wrote *I feel like a happy spider*. I love this line, because suddenly we realise that the poem isn't about a spider at all. It's about Sam.

Line five has two syllables, like the first line, and **sums up** the poem. You can repeat the first line. Or you can echo the first line. Sam chose to repeat the word *Spider*. I suggested that he choose a different word, especially as he had used the word spider in line four as well as line one, and I made some suggestions. Sam said, No – he wanted the word spider repeated. Well, this was Sam's poem, so I let him make the final decision. Here's the finished piece:

Spider
Teenie weenie
Spinning amazing webs
I feel like a happy spider
Spider

Sam Decie (aged 7)

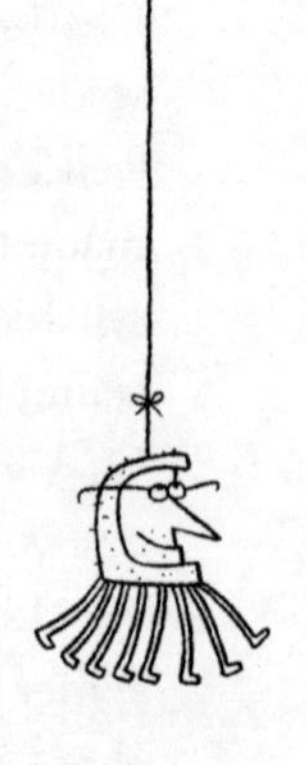

Most poets feel that it is better to stick with actual things rather than with abstract ideas or feelings when writing a **cinquain** (so write about an insect or a flower pot, rather than sadness or fear, for example).

Cinquains don't usually rhyme but you could use assonance (rhyming vowels) or alliteration (repeated consonants) to help make your cinquain more memorable.

To sum up:

Line 1 = two syllables. The subject of the poem.
Line 2 = four syllables. Describe the subject.
Line 3 = six syllables. Action.
Line 4 = eight syllables. Emotion. (Similes or metaphors work well here.)
Line 5 = two syllables. (Summing up or echoing line one.)

You can use the idea of counting in all sorts of ways when you write a poem. You could try writing a word cinquain – instead of counting syllables, count words.

Praying Mantis
In her yellow camouflage
She is sunbathing on the tent
It's relaxing doing nothing in the holiday sun
She's gone

You could do as Adelaide Crapsey did and make up your own form of poem. Choose a syllable pattern and give your form of poem a name, then try writing it.

I'll have a go... This is called a Stevens. A Stevens poem always has six lines and its syllables go 1, 3, 5, 5, 3, 1.

Hey!
Go for it!
Let's write a Stevens!
In a hundred years
I will have
fame!

I know, I know... not very good. Just make sure your syllables have a regular pattern – and try it. I'm sure your poem will be better than mine.

Mesostic Poems

Most young people are familiar with **acrostic** poems. You may well have learnt to write them at school, as it's very easy, and a fun way to write. All you do is write the subject of the poem down the left hand side of the page and then think of a phrase beginning with each of the letters that relates in some way to the object.

Acrostic poems go all the way back to Roman times. You can find examples in the Bible and in medieval literature.

Some **acrostic** poems are not very good but are just written for fun, or as coded love letters.

Message to Mary

I would like you to know that
Lettuces
Only grow in the summer and that
Vegetables are great!
Even cabbages, sometimes.
Maybe we could visit the
Allotment together?
Reply soon.
Yours, Billy.

It's difficult to write good or interesting **acrostics**. For one thing, whenever a line begins with a T it's so tempting to begin the phrase with the word the...

More interesting than **acrostics** are **mesostic** poems. The word **mesostic** was invented by the artist and composer John Cage.*

In a **mesostic** poem the subject of the poem reads roughly down the middle of the word, rather than down the left hand side. Here's how to write one.

First of all think of a subject. You can write mesostic poems about anything at all. Animals make good subjects. But I'm going to choose a time of the year. Right now, as I type this, it's the summer holidays. So *Summertime* will be my subject.

Next, on a piece of rough paper, write down as many words and phrases as you can about the subject. The more you can write the better. I've asked my grandson Sam to help again. This (over the page) is what we wrote:

*John Cage wrote a piece of music called 4'33" (often called 'Silence') in which a performer sits at the piano for four minutes and thirty-three seconds and doesn't play anything. A lot of people thought that this was silly and that John Cage was playing a joke. But actually the piece of music wasn't about silence. It was about the sound that the audience made when they were listening, the shuffling noises, and coughs, and whispers... and all the other sounds that go on around us all the time. John Cage was telling us that the most important thing in a musical performance wasn't about *playing* the music, but about *listening* to it.

Going on holiday
eating yummy ice creams
I like the warm weather
holidays can be boring
my best friend's gone to Spain
long walks along the beach
roller coaster rides
burying great grandpa in the sand
Swimming at St Jean
splashing water at Tara Dog
we made elderberry syrup
watching the lizards
buying sunglasses
camping in a tent with Grannie
I painted a picture of Paradise

It's good to have detail, not just general things, for example *swimming at St Jean* rather than just *swimming*.

Next you write the word down the middle of the page in capital letters.

S
U
M
M
E
R
T
I
M
E

Then you look through the list of words and phrases for those letters you need, which must appear roughly in the middle of the word. U can be quite a tricky letter, although we came up with several words with U in them. I thought the most interesting was *burying great grandpa in the sand* and I wanted to use it in the poem. But the U was too near the beginning of the line, so to make it appear nearer the middle, I changed the line. It's quite okay to change your words and phrases as you go along. In fact that's what working on a poem is all about. We ended up with this.

long walkS along the beach
where did we bUry Great Grandpa?
yumMy ice-creams
swimMing at St Jean
we made eldErberry syrup
roller coaster Rides
splashing water at Tara the dog
where Is grandpa buried?
hope we find hiM in time for supper
camping in a tEnt with grannie

I think **mesostics** are more fun than **acrostics**, and more of a challenge. They look better on the page too.

Now have a go at writing your own.

Advert Poems

To write an **advert poem** you must first have something to sell. How about getting rid of a few of your old toys? Your teddy bear? Come on, he's lost an eye and his arm is hanging by a thread! Or your bike? You're too big for it now anyway.

Or maybe you could think of selling something a little more interesting. How about your teacher? Your school caretaker? Or even your school?

Perhaps you could use your imagination here and think of some other things to sell, even though they're not really yours. Next-door's cat? A dragon? A dinosaur? How about selling Planet Earth? Maybe to someone who will take better care of it than we humans have done so far.

When you've decided what your poem is going to be about, you might like to do a little research. Have a look through a few magazines and see how advertisements are worded. People who are trying to sell you something are always very careful to tell you only good things. If they are trying to get you to buy a fizzy drink they tell you how delicious it is, how good fruit is for you, but they don't mention that their drink is full of sugar, which makes it not very good for you at all.

So the first things is to write down a list of all the good things about your 'product'. Try to think of as many reasons why someone might want to buy it as you can. You'll need to describe it too, in glowing terms if possible.

Then finally think about how much money you will sell it for. (Or maybe you might prefer to swap it for something else?) I'm going to try and sell my teddy bear. So… here's my list.

Eddie the Bear. He's very friendly and kind. He gets lost a lot but he's very brave. His arm was chewed off by Jasper, our Welsh Terrier, who thought he was a dog toy. He loves swimming, but doesn't like the washing machine much. He's good at sums, so can help with homework etc. He is soft and cuddly.

When I was writing my list I remembered that when I was about nine I thought I was too grown up for a teddy bear. And so I decided to use that idea in the poem.

When you're making a list, think of as many things as you can to go in the poem and write them down. You'll not use all of them, but good ideas will pop up. You might have some daft ideas, but they can turn into good poetry, so make sure you write them down as well, or they might get forgotten.

Finally, choose the best things from your list, and decide on the order to put them in.

For Sale – Eddie the Brave Bear

If you'd like a friend who's soft and cuddly,
Eddie's looking for a new home
He's very kind and good at sums!
So he can help you with your homework.
He needs someone to love him
(as our dog Jasper ripped his arm off)
He loves water (especially swimming
But not washing machines).
He got lost more than once.
But Jasper found him.
(This was a long time ago
before he lost his arm)
Please buy my teddy bear
as I am nearly nine and too old for him.
PS May I visit him sometimes please?

That's my first draft. Now I'll have a good look at the poem to see how I can improve it. I'll say it out loud to see how the words flow. The words need to have a good rhythm and this needs working on. I might make it shorter, or add words, perhaps add a rhyme or two.

After I've written the first draft of a poem I often leave it for a couple of days then come back to it to finish it off. This allows you to see the poem more clearly, and you can often spot ways that it could be improved.

Making a Cut-up Poem

There are all sorts of ways to write a **cut-up poem**. We'll start with a poem similar to the one I wrote earlier in this book in the style of William Carlos Williams.

Think of a place that you know really well. It could be your bedroom or your playroom. Maybe you have a shed in the garden. Or a tree house? How about a cellar or attic room (that could make a nice creepy and scary poem). Maybe there's a room in a relative's house – perhaps you visit your grandparents a lot. Or you could write about your classroom.

Next, on a sheet of A4 paper, write down as many words and phrases as you can about the room. You are going to be cutting the individual words out, so leave space around everything you write and don't write too small.

First of all write some describing words and phrases. When I was a boy I would visit my grandma and grandad. They lived next door. We had a pathway running along the backs of our terraced houses, so I could safely visit them any time I liked. This was over fifty years ago and so a lot of the things I remember will seem very old-fashioned now.

black and white TV
treadle sewing machine
small and gloomy room
sofa with piles of knitting
needlework magazine
clockwork clock with loud chime
grandad's large chair

I want to get some atmosphere and some emotion into the poem and so I'm going to think of the colours that the room reminds of, the smells and the feelings I had back then.

brown
dark
furniture polish
stale smells
damp
happy
excited

Finally a few things that I did in that room.

watched TV
played cards with grandad
putting salt and pepper on fish
eating unsliced bread

When you're finished, cut out **every single individual** word – even 'on' and 'with'. Don't cut out the phrases, cut out the words. By cutting out the words on my list, I have fifty pieces of paper each with a single word on.

Now think of a pattern for the words. The pattern you choose can be quite random. You can always adapt it to something else if you think of a better way to arrange your words. Don't forget, poets change lots of things as they go along in order to make their poem the best it can be.

Here are some suggestions for the number of words on a line:

2, 3, 2, 3, 2, 3, 2
4, 1, 4, 1, 4, 1
1, 2, 3, 4, 5, 5, 4, 3, 2, 1

You could have the words in pairs. Or you could adopt a **haiku**, **tanka** or **cinquain** syllable pattern.

Now muddle up your words. Shuffle them well. It's very important that you don't end up using the words in the order you wrote them down. If I wrote:

watched
black
and
white
television

then there wouldn't have been a lot of point going through the whole process of cutting out the words.
Now look for words that don't usually go together – odd

combinations of words – and put them together. You're looking to have fun with your words. And you don't have to use all the words. Just pick the ones you like best.

The poem doesn't have to make sense in the usual way we think of writing. But it should have meaning. And it should say something. Think of the pictures the Impressionists painted. Up close they look like splodgy messes, but from a distance they look realistic and quite beautiful.

You're trying to write a poem that gets to the essence of your subject matter; that suggests something rather than describes it accurately in detail. You don't have to make your reader's task easy. People enjoy having to work at understanding a poem.

Here's my attempt. I decided on nine lines in three groups of three, using one, two and then three words in a line:

Treadle
Fish chime
Watched unsliced room

Knitting
Clockwork grandad
Stale brown magazine

Excited
Chair pepper
Furniture white machine

And there you have it. I noticed that I had two words that rhymed: *magazine* and *machine*. So I put them at the ends of lines. Now I see that I could introduce some alliteration by putting *chair* and *chime* together. So I'll do that. I've also noticed that grandad is in the poem, but grandma isn't. So I'll swap one of the words for her. I've made the first letter of each line a capital. I like the way it looks. I'll need a title too. I might call it 'Room 1966'.

There are lots of other ways to write **cut-out poems.** Try cutting out lots of headlines from a newspaper and rearranging the words. You could end up with a topical, newsy poem like that. Or you could try using one of the colour supplements or a magazine. I once made a poem by cutting up titles and words in the *New Scientist*. You'll find some very obscure things there.

If you're into football, make a football poem by cutting up an old *FourFourTwo* or *Match!* or maybe you can find some old *Shoot* comics. (Maybe give the publication a mention in your title.) You can do the same no matter what your hobby or interest.

Good luck. And remember – have fun!

Top Eleven Tips for Writing Verse

I was once asked to write a list of my top tips for writing poems. The list has changed a bit over the years – but here are eleven suggestions that will definitely help you with your poetry.

1. Keep a notebook. This is the most important rule. You never know when an idea for a poem, or a word or phrase that suddenly takes your fancy, will present itself.

2. When you have an idea for a poem, write down the outline quickly. Don't worry about mistakes, your spelling, or if it turns out that you've written rubbish! No one need see your first draft. If you write lots, it's logical that some of your writing will be poor, some will be okay and every now and then something will be good, even very good!

3. Be tough on your own writing. Edit out the mediocre stuff. A brilliant three-line poem is much better than a wordy, boring, forty-line epic.

4. When you have cut out the not-so-good writing, read the rest of your poem out loud. (You could do this on a bus or in a café but I always find that somewhere private is best!) This will give you a feel for the poem's rhythm. The rhythm, or the beat, of a poem is very important. Poems don't have to rhyme

– but they do need to have a strong, free-flowing rhythm.

5. Look at the way your poem is constructed. Does it have verses? How are the lines grouped? In threes? In fours? What does your poem look like on the page? Try rearranging your poem in different ways until it feels right.

6. For some poets, rhyming comes quite naturally. And some poems seem to arrive in your head in rhyme. But some poets find rhyming more difficult. And some poems are better off without rhyme. If your poem does not rhyme at the end of the lines, you may still like to look for ways to add internal rhyme. Try using assonance – the rhyming of vowel sounds. And see how Shakespeare used rhythm in his plays. His blank verse has a strong beat. Although it doesn't all rhyme, he often rhymes the last two lines of a speech. It's a neat way to finish off a poem.

7. If your poem does rhyme, check that the final line doesn't sound contrived. If it does, you might try changing the rhyming lines around. Put the last line earlier. Swap it with the line it rhymes with. Try it – it sounds daft but it can produce a really good result.

8. Check for clichés. You want your poem to sound fresh and new. No 'cotton-wool clouds' or 'over the moon' or 'avoid it like the plague'. No 'I woke up and it was just a dream'. If you think you've heard or

seen a phrase, metaphor or simile before, then bin it and think up a better one.

9. As a general rule, poems take a LOT of work. (It's a rare and beautiful thing when a poem presents itself perfectly formed and ready to go.) Don't be afraid to cross things out, add things in, or change words or lines in any way. The goal of most poets is to produce a poem that says things simply and elegantly. And that can take some time to achieve.

10. When you think your poem is ready for the world to see, check it again! You are working with words, so please spell them properly. If you are not a great speller, ask for help if you need it. Poets (and authors) respect the words they use.

11. Finally, it is a good idea to show your poem to a trusted friend – someone who will not be scared to be critical, who will notice mistakes but who also will be positive. And then your poem is ready. Send it out into world, wish it luck, and get on with the next one.

And remember – writing poems should be fun. Play around with ideas, with words, with rhymes. Don't be afraid to cross things out or to change things. You may not grow up to be a poet, but being able to use words imaginatively and to communicate with words is a wonderful and very useful skill to have no matter what you do or where you go in life.

Acknowledgements

Cheryl Moskowitz, who showed me how to write cinquains.

All poems are by Roger Stevens unless otherwise attributed. The following poems are reproduced by kind permission of the poets or their estates:

'Not a Poem' by Sue Hardy Dawson; 'Cleaning my Room' by Jan Dean; 'People Love to Push Me' by Darren Sardelli; 'What is the World?' by James Carter; '8' by Coral Rumble; 'Class 4, Third Prize' by Ian Bland; 'Fat Cat' by Julie Rawlinson; 'Concrete Poems' and 'I Am a Free Verse' by John Foster; 'Gales of Laughter' by Chrissie Gittens; 'Tractor' and 'Deer Road' by John Rice; 'A Beggar Eats' by Steven Withrow; 'Fishy' by Trevor Parsons; 'Word Games' by Cheryl Moskowitz; 'I Wonder What 2 Do' by Jane Clarke; 'Bottom' and 'The Nasty Box' by Joshua Seigal. 'The Nasty Box' is based on 'The Magic Box' by Kit Wright (Macmillan Children's Books, 2013); 'Heron' and 'Riddle' by Liz Brownlee; 'Lonely Heart' and 'Ocean' by Graham Denton; 'Knocked Off' by Rupert Smith; 'Newts' and 'Party' by Philip Waddell; '10 Torn Messages' and 'Box of Frogs' by Celia Warren; 'A – Z' by Michaela Morgan; 'Edible Alphabet' by Angela Shavick; 'London A – Z' by Judith Nicholls; 'Fara Williams Forever' by Mike Johnson; 'Dragon' by Angela Topping; 'Doggerel' by Mike Barfield; 'Poetry Sale' by Bernard Young; 'Fragile Poem' by Eric Ode; 'Collage' by Laura Mucha; 'Leaves' by John H. Rice; 'Instead' by Brian Moses; 'Waiting for Dolphins' by Rita Borg; 'My Dog' and 'Spider' by Sam Decie; 'Mary Had a Little Lamp Post' by Michael Leigh; 'My Mum' and 'Castles' by Jill Pryor; 'Grief' by Debra Bertulis.

Roger Stevens would like to thank Macmillan Children's Books who first published his poems 'Happy and Sad', 'Drum Kit for Sale', 'September', 'Lesser Known Children's Games', 'Gherkin Car'.